Dear Parents and Educators,

Welcome to Penguin Young Readers! As parents and educators, you know that each child develops at his or her own pace—in terms of speech, critical thinking, and, of course, reading. Penguin Young Readers recognizes this fact. As a result, each Penguin Young Readers book is assigned a traditional easy-to-read level (1–4) as well as a Guided Reading Level (A–P). Both of these systems will help you choose the right book for your child. Please refer to the back of each book for specific leveling information. Penguin Young Readers features esteemed authors and illustrators, stories about favorite characters, fascinating nonfiction, and more!

Ladybug Girl
I Love You, Bingo

LEVEL 2

GUIDED READING LEVEL **G**

This book is perfect for a **Progressing Reader** who:
- can figure out unknown words by using picture and context clues;
- can recognize beginning, middle, and ending sounds;
- can make and confirm predictions about what will happen in the text; and
- can distinguish between fiction and nonfiction.

Here are some **activities** you can do during and after reading this book:
- Read the Pictures: Use the pictures in this book to tell the story. Have the child go through the book, retelling the story just by looking at the pictures.
- Sight Words: Sight words are frequently used words that readers know just by looking at them. These words are not "sounded out" or "decoded"; rather they are known instantly, on sight. Knowing these words helps children become efficient readers. As you are reading the story, have the child point out the sight words listed below.

and	her	play	this	with
every	is	they	too	you

Remember, sharing the love of reading with a child is the best gift you can give!

—Bonnie Bader, EdM
  Penguin Young Readers program

*Penguin Young Readers are leveled by independent reviewers apply...
and Gay Su Pinnell in *Matching Books to Readers: Using Leveled Books in Guided Reading*, Heinemann, ...

PENGUIN YOUNG READERS
An Imprint of Penguin Random House LLC

Copyright © 2015 by Jacky Davis and David Soman. All rights reserved. Published by Penguin Young Readers, an imprint of Penguin Random House LLC, 345 Hudson Street, New York, New York 10014. Manufactured in China.

Library of Congress Cataloging-in-Publication Data is available.

ISBN 978-0-448-48756-4 (pbk)   10 9 8 7 6 5 4 3 2 1
ISBN 978-0-448-48757-1 (hc)   10 9 8 7 6 5 4 3 2 1

Ladybug Girl

Ladybug Girl is a *New York Times* Best Seller

I Love You, Bingo

by David Soman and Jacky Davis
illustrated by Andy Grey

Penguin Young Readers
An Imprint of Penguin Random House

This is Lulu.

Lulu loves being Ladybug Girl.

She loves her dog, Bingo, too.

Every day, Ladybug Girl and
Bingo play together.
"I love to paint with you, Bingo,"
Ladybug Girl says.

Today, Ladybug Girl and Bingo
play outside.

They buzz around with bees.

They fly around with butterflies.

"I love to play with you, Bingo,"

Ladybug Girl says.

Ladybug Girl and Bingo run to
the woods.
Bingo gets there first.

Where are you, Bingo?

Bingo has found the Bug Squad.

They are in the fort.

Ladybug Girl is happy that

Bingo found her friends.

"I love to be with you and

my friends, Bingo," she says.

It is time to run!

The Bug Squad skips.

Bingo sits.

The Bug Squad climbs.

Bingo sleeps.

The Bug Squad spins.

Bingo rolls.

The Bug Squad flies.

Bingo runs.

"I love to run with you, Bingo!"

Ladybug Girl says.

Bingo sniffs.

Sniff, sniff, sniff!

Bingo runs off.

Where is Bingo going?

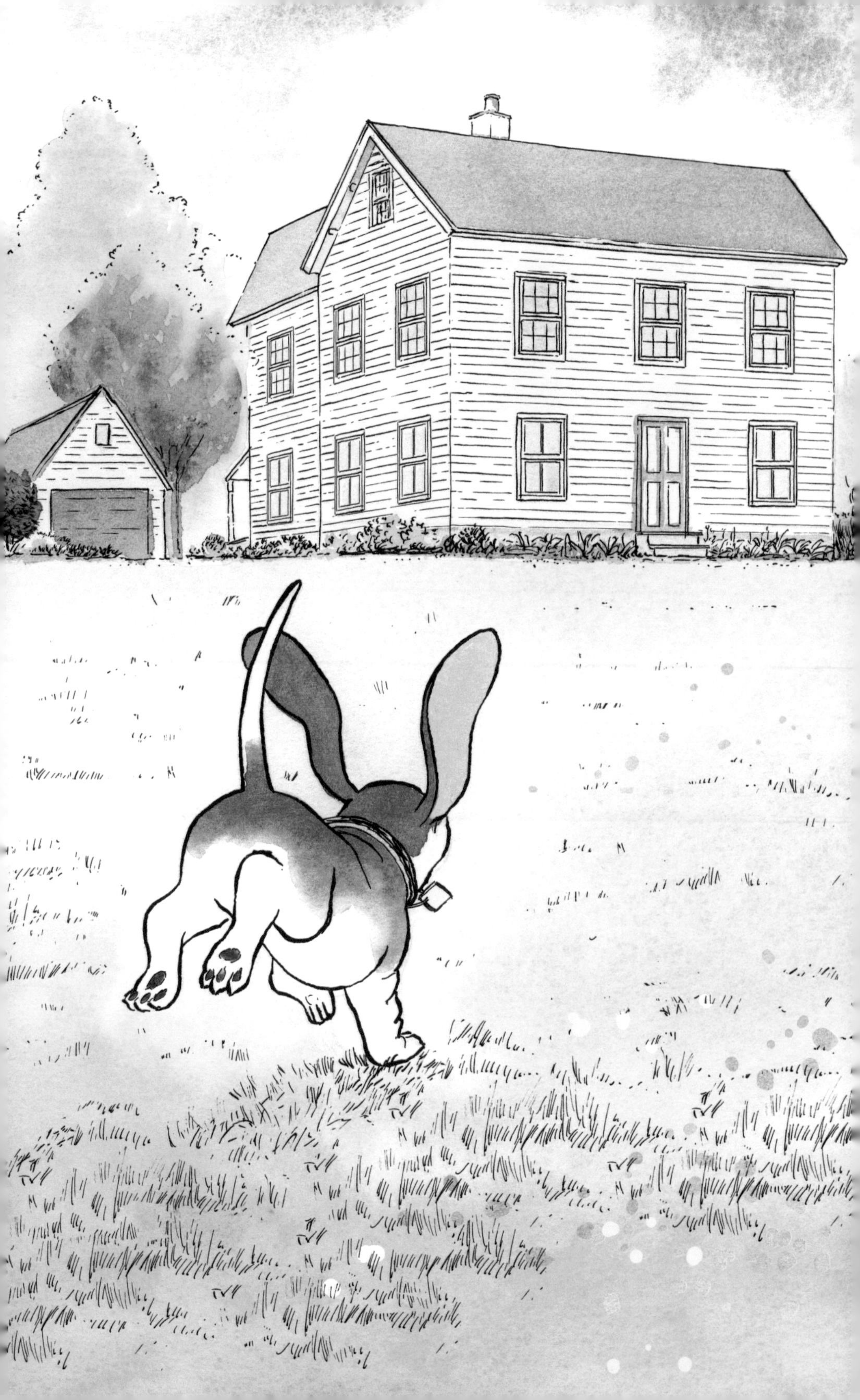

A picnic!

Bingo has found treats.

The Bug Squad gives Bingo

a hug.

Ladybug Girl gives Bingo

a really big hug.

"I love eating with you, Bingo!"

Ladybug Girl says.

The Bug Squad paints pictures.

They all have fun.

It is time for the Bug Squad
to go home.

Ladybug Girl and Bingo wave
good-bye.

Now it is time to take a bath.

Lulu and Bingo played

all day long.

"I love popping bubbles with you,

Bingo," Lulu says.

28

Lulu and Bingo had the best day.

They are now very tired.

Lulu and Bingo climb into bed.

"I love you, Bingo," Lulu says.